Dazzling DIGGERS

For Kate, Tim, Henry, and Angus—T.M.

KINGFISHER
Larousse Kingfisher Chambers Inc.
95 Madison Avenue
New York, New York 10016

First published in hardcover in 1997
First published in paperback in 2000
2 4 6 8 10 9 7 5 3 1 (HC)
2 4 6 8 10 9 7 5 3 1 (PB)

1TR/0500/TWP/FR/AMA170

LIBRARY OF CONGRESS CATALOGING-IN-PUBLICATION DATA
Mitton, Tony.
Dazzling diggers / Tony Mitton (author) : Ant Parker
(illustrator). — 1st American ed.
p. cm.
Summary: Animals operate digging machines that scoop, lift, move
rubble, squish through mud, and help buildings tower up tall.
[1. Excavating machinery—Fiction. 2. Animals—Fiction.
3. Stories in rhyme.] I. Parker, Ant. ill. II. Title.
PZ8.3.M685Daz 1997
[E]—DC21   97-9944   CIP AC

ISBN 0-7534-5105-0 (HC)
ISBN 0-7534-5304-5 (PB)

Printed in Singapore

Dazzling
DIGGERS

Tony Mitton and
Ant Parker

Lunch box

KINGFISHER

NEW YORK

Diggers are noisy, strong, and big.

Diggers can carry and push and dig.

Scoop

Diggers have shovels to scoop and lift,

blades that bulldoze, shunt, and shift.

Diggers have buckets to gouge out ground,

breakers that crack and smash and pound.

Diggers move rubble and rocks and soil,

so diggers need drinks of diesel oil.

Some have tires and some have tracks.

Some keep steady with legs called jacks.

Tires and tracks grip hard as they travel,

squish through mud and grind through gravel.

Diggers go scrunch and squelch and slosh.

This dirty digger needs a really good wash.

Diggers can bash and crash and break,

make things crumble, shiver, and shake.

Diggers can heave and hoist and haul.

Diggers help buildings tower up tall.

Drivers park neatly, down on the site.

And then they all go home. Goodnight!

Digger parts

levers

these control different
parts of the digger

jack

this holds the
digger steady when
it is lifting or digging

tire

this helps the wheel to
grip the ground and get
the digger moving

breaker

this is for cracking
concrete or lumps
of rock

bucket

this is for digging
and scooping out

piston

this is a strong pump
that makes parts of
the digger move aroun

tracks

these help the digger
to travel over slippery
or bumpy ground

blade

this is for knocking
down and pushing along